Dance Class

Béka • Writer

Crip • Artist

Maëla Cosson • Colorist

New York

Dance Class Graphic Novels available from PAPERCUTZ

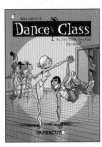

#1 "So, You Think You Can Hip-Hop?"

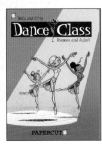

#2 "Romeos and Juliet"

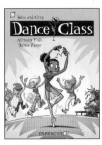

#3 "African Folk Dance Fever"

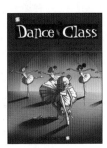

#4 "A Funny Thing Happened on the Way to Paris..."

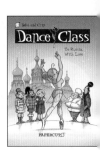

#5 "To Russia, With Love"

#6 "A Merry Olde Christmas"

#7 "School Night Fever"

#8 "Snow White and the Seven Dwarves"

#9 "Dancing in the Rain"

#10 "Letting It Go"

DANCE CLASS graphic novels are available for $10.99 each only in hardcover. Available from booksellers everywhere. You can also order online from papercutz.com or call 1-800-886-1223, Monday through Friday, 9 - 5 EST. MC, Visa, and AmEx accepted. To order by mail, please add $5.00 for postage and handling for first book ordered, $1.00 for each additional book and make check payable to NBM Publishing. Send to: Papercutz, 160 Broadway, Suite 700, East Wing, New York, NY 10038.

DANCE CLASS graphic novels are also available digitally wherever e-books are sold.

Papercutz.com

Studio Danse [Dance Class]
by Béka and Crip
©2017 BAMBOO ÉDITION.
www.bamboo.fr
English translation and all other editorial material © 2020 by Papercutz.

www.papercutz.com

DANCE CLASS #10
"Letting It Go"
BÉKA — Writer
CRIP — Artist
MAËLA COSSON — Colorist
MARK MCNABB — Production
JOE JOHNSON — Translation
WILSON RAMOS JR. — Lettering
JEFF WHITMAN — Editor
JIM SALICRUP
Editor-in-Chief

Special thanks to
CATHERINE LOISELET

ISBN: 978-1-5458-0432-2

Printed in Malaysia
November 2020

Papercutz books may be purchased for business or promotional use. For information on bulk purchases please contact Macmillan Corporate and Premium Sales Department at (800) 221-794 x5442.

Distributed by Macmillan
First Papercutz Printing

CLIC

CLIC

JULIE! JULIE! ARE YOU ASLEEP?

NOT ANYMORE.

WHAT'S GOING ON, *CAPUCINE?* SOMETHING BOTHERING YOU?

I DIDN'T DANCE TODAY!

OH? ME EITHER. THAT HAPPENS SOMETIMES...

IN MY BOOK, THEY SAY THAT TO BECOME A PRIMA BALLERINA, YOU HAVE TO DANCE EVERY DAY!

HMMM. THAT'S TRUE.

OKAY. IT'S NOT MIDNIGHT YET!

AND?

WE CAN STILL DANCE BEFORE TOMORROW COME ON, CAPUCINE!

POF
POF POF
POF POF POF

POF
POF POF
POF POF
POF POF

POF
POF
POF

DO YOU HEAR THAT NOISE?

IT'S NOTHING. YOU HAVE THE GIRLS ON YOUR MIND. GO BACK TO SLEEP.

HEE-HEE! THAT WAS AWESOME!

AND IT REALLY DOES YOU GOOD.

DO YOU THINK *LUCIE* AND *ALIA* GOT TO DANCE TODAY TOO?

LUCIE, YES. SHE WAS DANCING WITH JOY IN THE COURTYARD AFTER GETTING A GOOD GRADE IN LANGUAGE ARTS.

AND ALIA... I'M SURE SHE WILL, AT LEAST IN HER DREAMS.

INDEED...

POW

!

BAM

OW!

THE NEXT DAY AT THE DANCE SCHOOL...

Dance Class

CARLA'S KEEPING YOU FROM DANCING EVEN IN YOUR DREAMS? AREN'T YOU EXAGGERATING A LITTLE, ALIA?

I SWEAR! SHE TOOK MY PLACE ON STAGE AND--

!!

PoF

OOPS! SORRY!

!

GLOUB GLOUB

WHAT DID I TELL YOU? SHE'S CAPABLE OF ANYTHING!

NO, ALIA. I'M SURE IT WAS SIMPLE CLUMSINESS...

WAP

OH, SORRY.

I'D LIKE TO BELIEVE YOU, LUCIE, BUT I HIGHLY DOUBT IT.

EVERYONE HERE? PERFECT!

AS YOU KNOW, FOR THE END OF THE YEAR, WE'RE REHEARSING A BALLET ADAPTED FROM THE *ANDERSEN* FAIRY TALE "THE SNOW QUEEN"!

IN FACT, *NATHALIA*, OUR SEAMSTRESS, HAS JUST FINISHED THE COSTUME FOR THE LEADING ROLE... THE SNOW QUEEN. THE DRESS IS SO BEAUTIFUL WE JUST HAD TO SHOW IT TO YOU...

MARY WENT TO GET IT. SHE SHOULDN'T BE LONG NOW...

I'D RATHER THE STUDENTS NOT SEE IT YET! I'M NOT COMPLETELY SATISFIED AND--

DON'T WORRY, NATHALIA. THIS DRESS IS PERFECT.

HELLO, GIRLS! READY TO SEE THE MOST BEAUTIFUL COSTUME EVER CREATED FOR A BALLET?

DON'T LOOK! DON'T LOOK!

TAH-DAH!

WOOOOOOW!

IT'S WONDERFUL!

BRAVO, NATHALIA!

IT LOOKS LIKE IT'S FROM A MAGAZINE.

IT'S SO MODERN YOU COULD EVEN WEAR IT IN TOWN.

OR FOR A PARTY!

MEH. I THINK IT'S BORING.

THAT'S NOT FAIR, CARLA!

YOU'RE SAYING THAT BECAUSE YOU DIDN'T GET THE BALLET'S LEADING ROLE!

JULIE'S THE ONE WHO'LL DANCE THE SNOW QUEEN!

UH... NOTHING'S REALLY DECIDED, YOU KNOW. I HAVE TO BE UP TO THE TASK...

GIRLS, WE WANTED TO SHOW YOU THIS COSTUME TO MOTIVATE YOU BEFORE STARTING REHEARSALS... JUST KNOW THEY'LL ALL BE AS LOVELY AS THAT ONE!

SO, GET TO WORK NOW. COME INTO THE MIDDLE, PLEASE!

YES, MISS ANNE.

STILL, I DON'T THINK THIS DRESS IS ENTIRELY FINISHED.

I TOTALLY AGREE.

AN HOUR LATER...

ARRIÈRE CROISÉE POSITION...

RAISED CROISÉ DEVANT!

GOOD JOB! THAT'LL BE ALL FOR TODAY, YOUNG LADIES.

YOU'RE DOING SO WELL WITH THE POINTES, JULIE. YOU'LL BE WONDERFUL AS THE SNOW QUEEN.

THAT'S KIND, LUCIE. BUT FOR NOW, I'M MORE LIKE THE BLISTER QUEEN!

!

WOOOOOW!

WHAT AN AWESOME DRESS!

COSTUME STORAGE

THAT WILL NO DOUBT BE YOUR SISTER'S COSTUME IN THIS YEAR'S BALLET, CAPUCINE.

SHE'S SO LUCKY! I WISH I WERE BIGGER TO WEAR THIS, TOO...

ONE DAY, PERHAPS. I'LL PUT IT AWAY IN THE MEANTIME. GOOD AFTERNOON, YOUNG LADIES.

GOOD AFTERNOON, MISS ANNE!

THIS DRESS REALLY IS BEAUTIFUL...

THIS SNOW QUEEN BALLET'S PROMISING TO BE WONDERFUL. FULL OF FRESHNESS!

CLIK CLAK

AND THE LEAD ROLE DESERVES A STAR.

MANAGEMENT

A SNOW STAR! HEE-HEE!

MANAGEMENT

SHE'S GONE.

I CAN GO GET THE KEY.

THAT NIGHT, MORE THAN ONE STUDENT DREAMS SHE'S THE SNOW QUEEN...

SMMEK

...AND NOT JUST THE STUDENTS...

THE NEXT DAY...

WE BETTER HURRY, ALIA. WE MIGHT BE LATE FOR DANCE.

WE SHOULD BE OKAY.

THERE'S ONLY A SHOE STORE THE REST OF THE WAY.

SOON AFTER...

OH! THERE YOU FINALLY ARE!

YOU'RE JUST IN TIME. CLASS STARTS IN TWO MINUTES.

⸲PFFF!⸱ APART FROM YOU, LUCIE, NOBODY WOULD'VE NOTICED THEIR ABSENCE!

WE'RE LUCKY MISS ANNE HASN'T ARRIVED YET. THAT'S WEIRD, TOO. SHE'S ALWAYS EARLY...

OH! THERE SHE IS!

YOUNG LADIES, *IT'S A CATASTROPHE!*

I JUST WENT BY THE COSTUME STORAGE, AND THE SNOW QUEEN'S DRESS ISN'T THERE ANYMORE! *IT'S GONE!*

WHAT?! BUT HOW IS THAT POSSIBLE?

DON'T OVERTHINK IT! CARLA'S THE ONE WHO DID IT!

YES! WE SAW HOW JEALOUS SHE WAS OF JULIE AND THE DRESS.

AND SHE'S ALWAYS PLAYING DIRTY TRICKS.

!

BUT?... BUT?... NO WAY! IT'S NOT ME!

SURELY YOU'RE NOT GOING TO DENY YOU WERE TRYING YOUR BEST TO TEAR IT AWAY FROM ME IN MY LATEST DREAM!

!?

CALM DOWN, YOUNG LADIES. WE'RE NOT ACCUSING ANYONE WITHOUT PROOF. I'LL SEE TO THIS MATTER AFTER CLASS...

YOU'LL START OFF WITH A FEW BAR EXERCISES, THEN YOU'LL GO OUT TO THE MIDDLE...

DÉGAGÉ ON A COUP-DE-PIED!

FOUETTÉ!...

BATTEMENT FRAPPÉ!...

THAT'S EXACTLY WHAT I'D LIKE TO DO TO THE ONE WHO STOLE THAT DRESS!

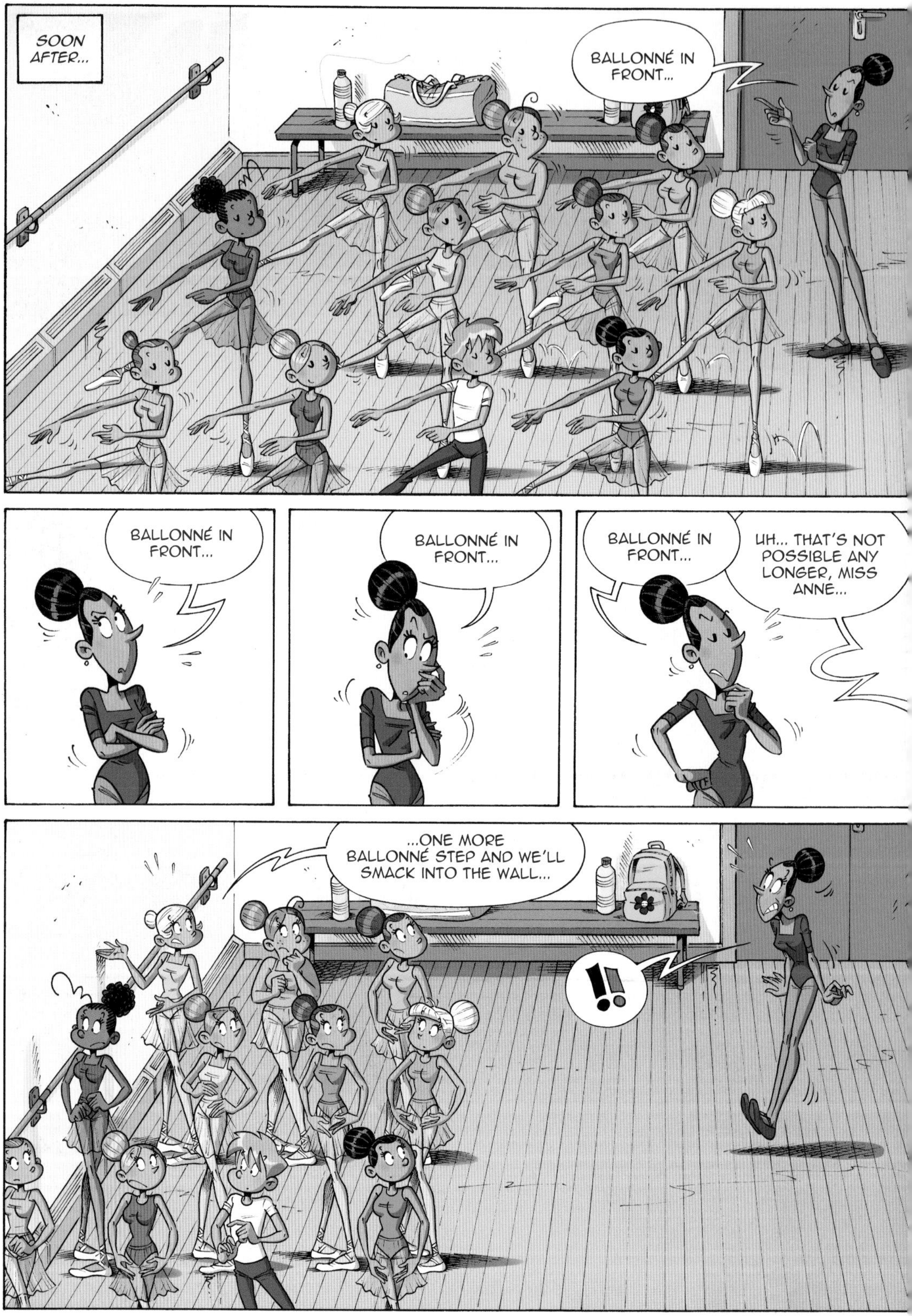
SOON AFTER...
BALLONNÉ IN FRONT...
BALLONNÉ IN FRONT...
BALLONNÉ IN FRONT...
BALLONNÉ IN FRONT...
UH... THAT'S NOT POSSIBLE ANY LONGER, MISS ANNE...
...ONE MORE BALLONNÉ STEP AND WE'LL SMACK INTO THE WALL...
!!

OH, SORRY! MY MIND WAS ELSEWHERE. THAT MISSING DRESS IS DISTRACTING ME...

WE'D BETTER STOP THERE TODAY. I MUST ALERT THE OTHER TEACHERS...

A FEW MOMENTS LATER...

!?

WHY ARE YOU ALL LOOKING AT ME LIKE THAT?

CARLA, GIVE BACK THAT DRESS!

I TOLD YOU I WASN'T THE ONE WHO TOOK IT!

YOU KNOW, IF THE DRESS ISN'T FOUND, THE SHOW WON'T TAKE PLACE, AND NOBODY WILL SEE YOU DANCE!

!!

THAT'S TRUE! I HADN'T THOUGHT OF THAT!

THAT'S HORRIBLE!

DON'T YOU REALIZE WE ABSOLUTELY HAVE TO FIND THAT DRESS?!

!

CALM DOWN, CARLA! I'M SURE MISS ANNE WILL CLEAR UP THE MYSTERY...

AND WITHOUT STRANGLING ANYONE EITHER!

HMM... THERE'S NO DOUBT MISS ANNE IS THE BEST CLASSICAL DANCE TEACHER, BUT I'M NOT SURE SHE'S A GREAT DETECTIVE.

I'LL HAVE TO TAKE CHARGE OF THINGS ONCE AGAIN. WITH MY SUPERIOR INTELLIGENCE, I'LL QUICKLY UNMASK THE CULPRIT, AND ALL THE OTHERS WILL HAVE TO APOLOGIZE FOR UNJUSTLY ACCUSING ME!

IT'LL BE A BIG MOMENT! I'LL FILM IT WITH MY CELLPHONE.

OKAY, I DON'T HAVE A MOMENT TO WASTE. I'LL START MY INVESTIGATION RIGHT AWAY.

THE KEY TO THE COSTUME STORAGE IS IN MISS ANNE'S OFFICE, SO ANYONE COULD EASILY COME GET IT... WHICH MEANS THE WHOLE SCHOOL IS A SUSPECT!

NOW LET'S SEE IF THE THIEF DIDN'T LEAVE ANY TRACES BEHIND...

AH-HA!

A MEASURING TAPE AND A BARRETTE!

THE MEASURING TAPE MUST BE NATHALIA'S. SHE MUST HAVE FORGOTTEN IT ONE DAY WHEN SHE CAME TO DO A FEW TOUCH-UPS ON THE COSTUMES...

THE BARRETTE, HOWEVER, IS A REAL CLUE. IT MUST BELONG TO ONE OF THE DANCE CLASS KIDS!

IN FACT, THEY'LL SOON HAVE CLASS WITH MARY. HEH-HEH! I'LL GO SPY ON THEM ON THE SLY.

SO, HAVE YOU FOUND YOUR OUTFIT FOR MY BIRTHDAY PARTY?

YES! IT'S FABULOUS!

I WON'T TELL YOU WHAT IT LOOKS LIKE! I... I'D RATHER KEEP IT SECRET.

BUT I'M SURE YOU'LL ALL BE TOTALLY JEALOUS. IT'S THE *PRETTIEST* OUTFIT!

!!

THAT KID'S THE ONE WHO STOLE THE SNOW QUEEN'S DRESS FOR HER BIRTHDAY OUTFIT! THAT'S WHY SHE DOESN'T WANT TO TELL JULIE'S SISTER.

WHAT'S MORE, SHE'S WEARING EXACTLY THE SAME BARRETTE I JUST FOUND IN THE COSTUME STORAGE! SHE MUST HAVE DROPPED IT WHEN SHE TOOK THE DRESS.

IN THE NEXT CLASS, I'LL REVEAL EVERYTHING TO MISS ANNE AND THE OTHER STUDENTS.

I'LL BE CLEARED OF ALL SUSPICION.

IT'LL BE MY TRIUMPH!

I KNEW IT!

?!

NOW THAT SHE HAS THE DRESS, SHE'S TRAINING IN SECRET TO TAKE OVER JULIE'S ROLE!

YES, BUT HER CHOREOGRAPHY IS TERRIBLE!

!

THAT NIGHT...

CLIC

CLAP CLAP

BRAVO!

WHAT A DANCER!

CLAP CLAP CLAP

WHAT A LOVELY DREAM.

I'LL HAVE TO TALK ABOUT THIS WITH MISS ANNE. MAYBE THERE'S SOME WAY TO ADD A SCENE LIKE THAT INTO THE SNOW QUEEN BALLET...

SHE WON'T BE ABLE TO REFUSE ME ANYTHING SINCE I'VE DISCOVERED WHO STOLE THE DRESS.

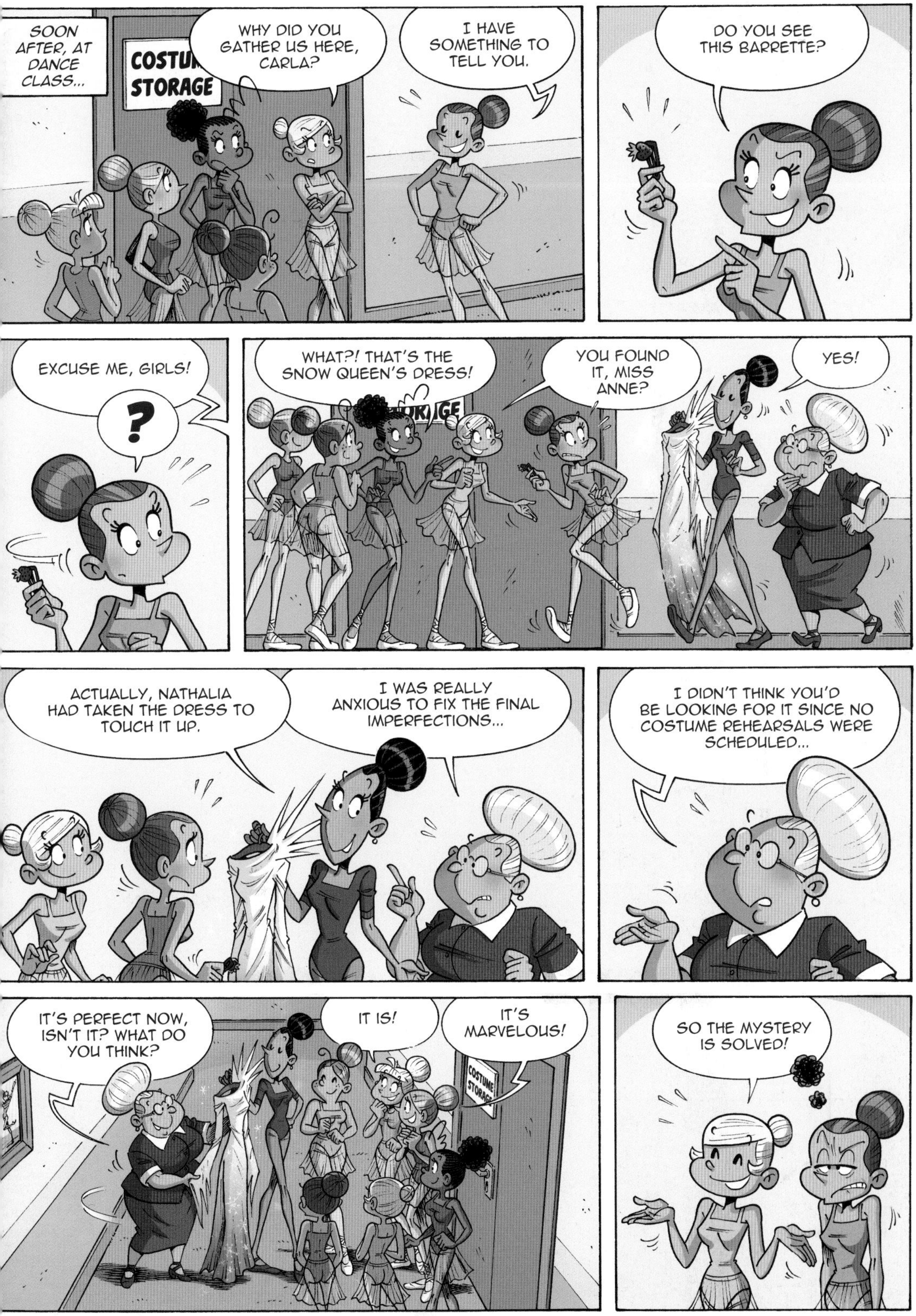
SOON AFTER, AT DANCE CLASS...
COSTUME STORAGE
WHY DID YOU GATHER US HERE, CARLA?
I HAVE SOMETHING TO TELL YOU.
DO YOU SEE THIS BARRETTE?
EXCUSE ME, GIRLS!
?
WHAT?! THAT'S THE SNOW QUEEN'S DRESS!
YOU FOUND IT, MISS ANNE?
YES!
ACTUALLY, NATHALIA HAD TAKEN THE DRESS TO TOUCH IT UP.
I WAS REALLY ANXIOUS TO FIX THE FINAL IMPERFECTIONS...
I DIDN'T THINK YOU'D BE LOOKING FOR IT SINCE NO COSTUME REHEARSALS WERE SCHEDULED...
IT'S PERFECT NOW, ISN'T IT? WHAT DO YOU THINK?
IT IS!
IT'S MARVELOUS!
COSTUME STORAGE
SO THE MYSTERY IS SOLVED!

I'LL PUT THE DRESS SAFELY AWAY IN THE COSTUME STORAGE RIGHT NOW.

COSTUME STORAGE

SORRY, CARLA! WE WERE WRONG TO ACCUSE YOU.

WE'RE ALL SORRY.

ANYWAY, WHAT WERE YOU WANTING TO TELL US?

UH WELL... UH...

!

OOOH! YOU FOUND MY BARRETTE!

I WAS LOOKING EVERYWHERE FOR IT. I'D THOUGHT I'D LOST IT WHILE HELPING MISS ANNE TO STRAIGHTEN UP THE COSTUME STORAGE ROOM.

!

THAT'S IT!... UH... I'D FOUND THAT BARRETTE AND WANTED TO KNOW WHOSE IT WAS.

THANKS!

GRUMBLE!

?

CARLA WILL NEVER CHANGE. EVEN WHEN SHE DOES SOMETHING NICE FOR SOMEONE, SHE GRUMBLES.

IT'S A TOTAL FAILURE!

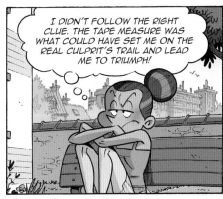

I DIDN'T FOLLOW THE RIGHT CLUE. THE TAPE MEASURE WAS WHAT COULD HAVE SET ME ON THE REAL CULPRIT'S TRAIL AND LEAD ME TO TRIUMPH!

AND WHAT'S WORSE, I'VE SPENT SO MUCH TIME POUTING, I'M NOW LATE FOR CLASS!

UH... SORRY, MISS ANNE! I... UH...

IT'S NO USE SAYING YOU'RE SORRY, CARLA! BEING LATE IS UNACCEPTABLE. JUST IMAGINE IF IT WERE A PERFORMANCE...

THAT'S WHY I NEVER ENTRUST LEADING ROLES TO STUDENTS WHO AREN'T PUNCTUAL!

MY SCHEME TOTALLY FLOPPED. ALL BECAUSE OF THAT STUPID BRAT WITH HER BARRETTE!

I WONDER WHAT DRESS SHE WAS TALKING ABOUT IF IT WASN'T THE SNOW QUEEN ONE?

-21-

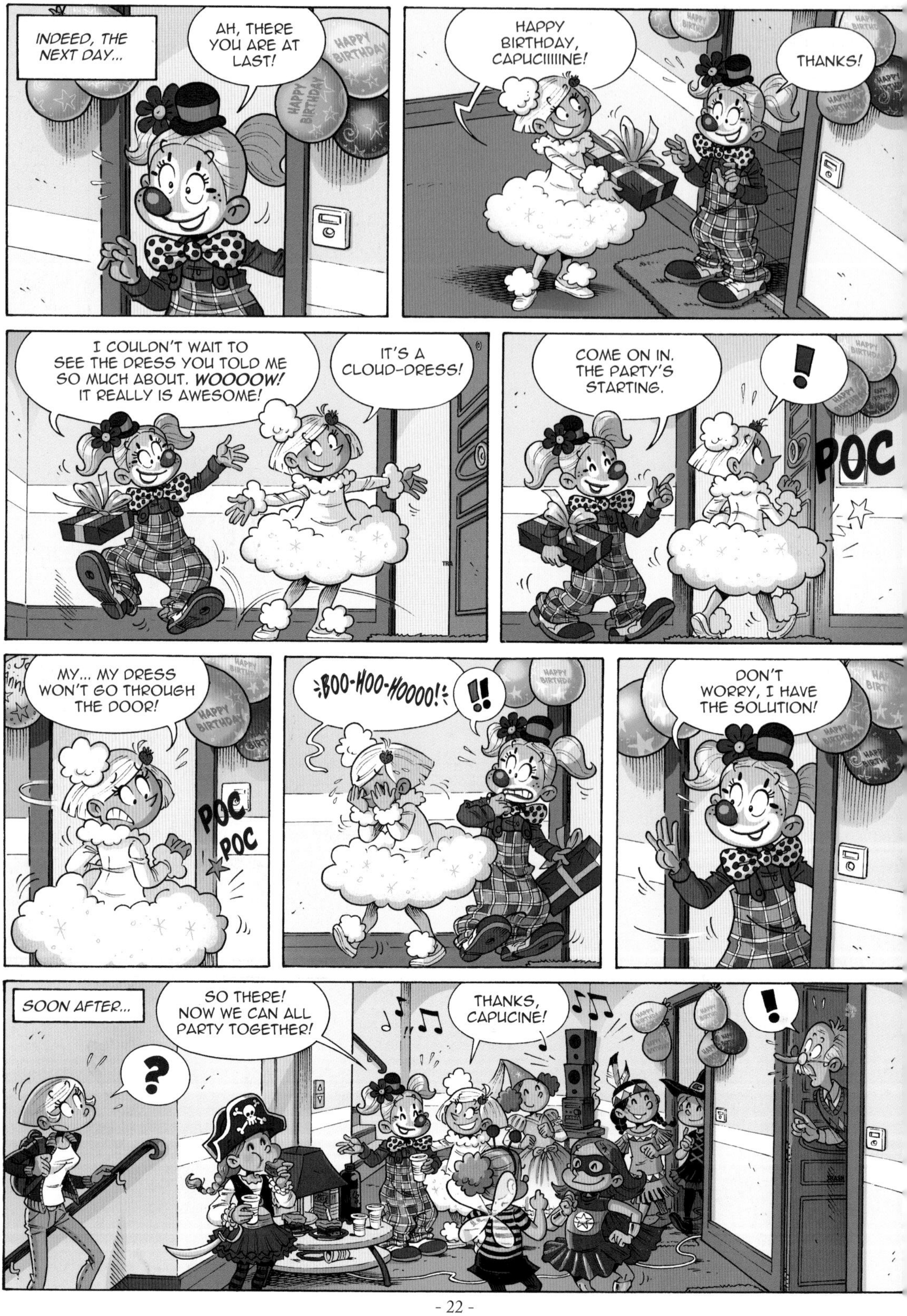
INDEED, THE NEXT DAY...
AH, THERE YOU ARE AT LAST!
HAPPY BIRTHDAY
HAPPY BIRTHDAY, CAPUCIIIIIINE!
THANKS!
I COULDN'T WAIT TO SEE THE DRESS YOU TOLD ME SO MUCH ABOUT. WOOOOW! IT REALLY IS AWESOME!
IT'S A CLOUD-DRESS!
COME ON IN. THE PARTY'S STARTING.
!
POC
MY... MY DRESS WON'T GO THROUGH THE DOOR!
POC
POC
BOO-HOO-HOOOO!
!!
DON'T WORRY, I HAVE THE SOLUTION!
SOON AFTER...
?
SO THERE! NOW WE CAN ALL PARTY TOGETHER!
THANKS, CAPUCINE!
!

THE FOLLOWING MONDAY...

MISS ANNE'S ALREADY MAD AT ME ABOUT BEING LATE, THE DRESS MUSTN'T DISAPPEAR AGAIN, TOO. I'D BE ACCUSED AGAIN. IT WOULD BE A CATASTROPHE!

I KNOW! I'LL REGULARLY GO TAKE A LOOK IN THE COSTUME STORAGE TO MAKE SURE EVERYTHING'S OKAY.

SHORTLY THEREAFTER...

GOOD. THE DRESS IS IN ITS PLACE.

?

THE NEXT DAY...

STILL THERE.

?

AND THE FOLLOWING DAY...

THE DRESS IS STILL IN ITS PLACE, AND THE DOOR TO THE ROOM IS TIGHTLY LOCKED.

?

CLONC CLONC

I CAN REST ASSURED! NOW I JUST HAVE TO WAIT FOR MISS ANNE TO FORGET ABOUT ME BEING LATE, AND I'LL BE GOOD.

COME ON, CARLA, CLASS HAS ALREADY BEGUN.

!!

NEXT TIME, TRY TO BE ON TIME INSTEAD OF HANGING IN THE HALLWAY!

GREAT! NOW I GOT TO WAIT FOR BOTH MISS ANNE AND *MARY* TO FORGET ABOUT ME BEING LATE, AND I'LL BE GOOD.

AT THE END OF THE WEEK, AFTER A CLASS OF CLASSICAL DANCE...

OKAY! WE'LL STOP THERE, YOUNG LADIES.

AAAH! IT'S GOOD TO CATCH YOUR BREATH!

≈PFFFFF!≈

I HAVE TO LEAVE SOON FOR A MEETING, LUCIE. COULD YOU PUT THESE SPATS AWAY IN THE COSTUME STORAGE?

OF COURSE, MISS ANNE!

COSTUME STORAGE

?

!!

GIRLS, I WAS IN THE STORAGE AND...

!

THE SNOW QUEEN DRESS HAS DISAPPEARED AGAIN!

!

WHAT?!

BOP

OWW!

THAT WAS A HARD KNOCK!

CARLA, THIS TIME YOU CAN'T SAY YOU HAD NOTHING TO DO WITH IT!

!

I SAW YOU POKING AROUND THE COSTUME STORAGE THE OTHER DAY.

ME TOO!

AND I SAW YOU TRYING TO OPEN THE DOOR.

!!

BUT! BUT! I SWEAR TO YOU I'M INNOCENT!

STOP TELLING US STORIES!

IT'S SATURDAY MORNING. IF YOU HAVEN'T BROUGHT THE DRESS BACK BY MONDAY, WE'RE TELLING THE TEACHERS!

!

THIS IS REALLY SO UNFAIR!

BUT I'M NOT GOING TO GET PUSHED AROUND! I'M GOING TO START A NEW INVESTIGATION AND, THIS TIME, I'LL FIND THE REAL CULPRIT!

YOU OKAY, ALIA?

YES! NOW I UNDERSTAND WHY MISS ANNE ALWAYS TELLS US TO BE CAREFUL WHEN HITTING THE BAR!

DRESSING ROOM!

SOON AFTER...

HMMMM...

COSTUME STORAGE

I WONDER WHO COULD'VE STOLEN THAT DRESS WHEN I KEPT WATCH THE WHOLE WEEK!

COS STORAGE

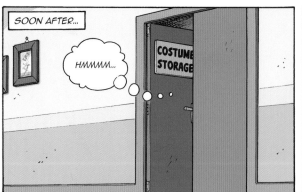

HEY! *SAM'S* DJEMBE!

COSTUME STORAGE

HMMMM... I'M SURE IT WASN'T THERE THE LAST TIME I CAME BY.

COSTUME STORAGE

IT'S WEIRD THAT SAM WOULD STEAL A DRESS, BUT IT'S THE ONLY CLUE I HAVE. I'LL GO SPY ON HIM RIGHT AWAY...

COSTUME STORAGE

YOU KNOW, *FATOU*, I FINALLY HAVE A BIRTHDAY PRESENT FOR MY GIRLFRIEND.

OH? WHAT IS IT?

A DRESS! BUT NOT JUST ANY DRESS...

IT'S UNIQUE! MAGNIFICENT! THERE ISN'T ANOTHER ONE LIKE IT!

!!

I'M SURE I'M NOT MISTAKEN THIS TIME. I HAVE THE CULPRIT!

HEH-HEH! I'LL TURN HIM IN ON MONDAY.

I CAN'T WAIT TILL THEN!

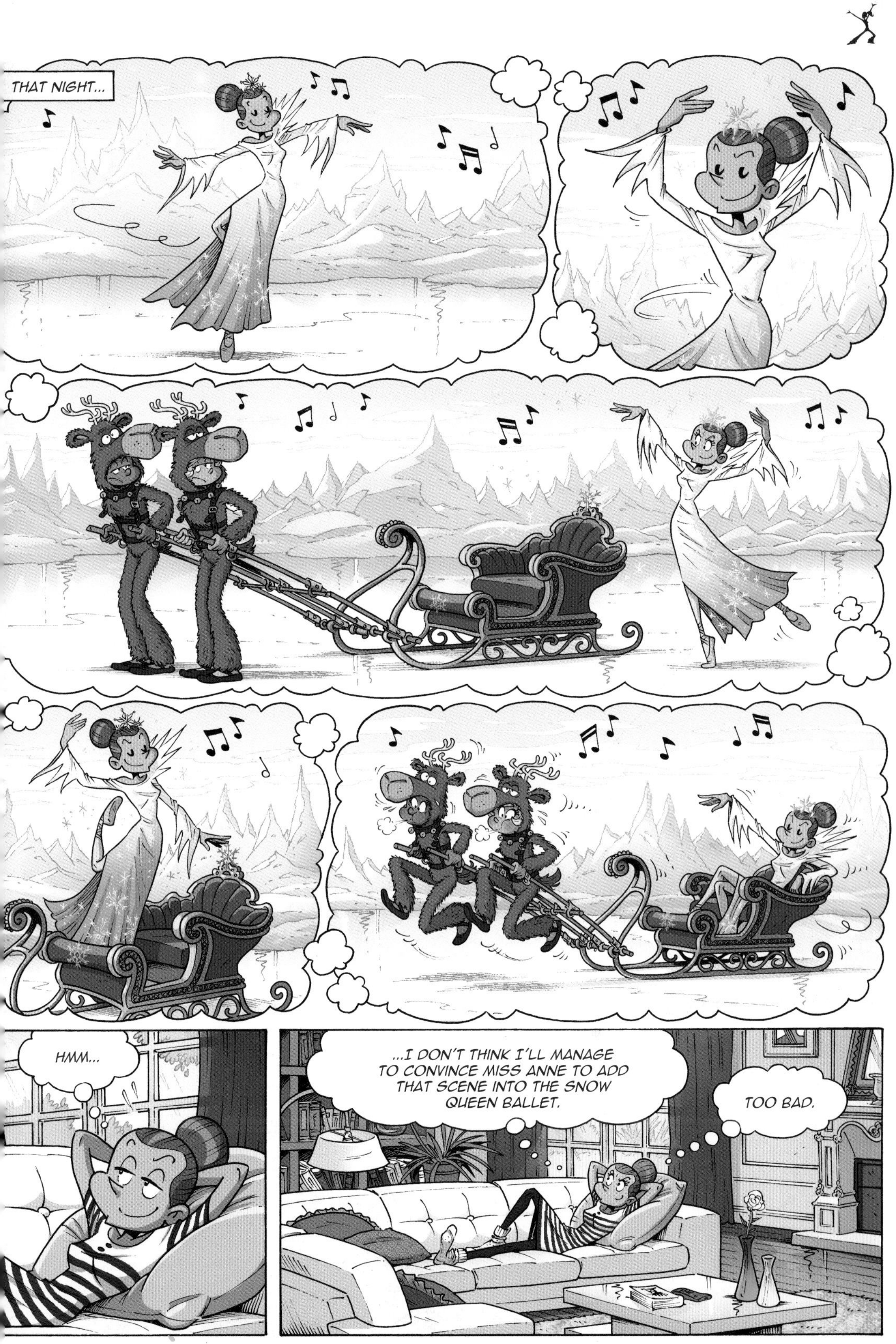
THAT NIGHT...
HMM...
...I DON'T THINK I'LL MANAGE TO CONVINCE MISS ANNE TO ADD THAT SCENE INTO THE SNOW QUEEN BALLET.
TOO BAD.

ON MONDAY...

AH, THERE YOU ARE, CARLA! WE WERE WAITING FOR YOU.

SO, DID YOU BRING BACK THE DRESS?

NOPE!

AS I TOLD YOU, I'M NOT THE ONE WHO STOLE IT. BUT I KNOW WHO THE CULPRIT IS.

OH?

AND WHO IS IT?

IT'S--

MARY!

?!

OH! SO YOU'RE THE ONE WHO HAD THE DRESS?

!

YES, I BORROWED IT TO GO TO A WEDDING THIS WEEKEND. I CAUSED A SENSATION, I CAN ASSURE YOU.

OKAY! SEE YOU, GIRLS. I'LL QUICKLY GO PUT IT BACK IN THE COSTUME STORAGE...

NOBODY MUST START IMAGINING IT'S DISAPPEARED AGAIN! HEE-HEE!

!

!

!

WE WRONGLY ACCUSED YOU AGAIN, CARLA. WE'RE ALL SORRY.

YOU KNEW IT WAS MARY AND DIDN'T WANT TO TELL ON HER. THAT WAS VERY KIND OF YOU.

UH... YES. I... I'M LIKE THAT.

COME ON, LET'S QUICKLY GET READY FOR THE AFRICAN DANCE CLASS.

⸮WHEW!⸮ THAT WAS CLOSE! I NEARLY EMBARRASSED MYSELF BY ACCUSING SAM...

BUT I DO WONDER WHAT DRESS HE WAS TALKING ABOUT?

SOON AFTER...

HEY! YOU'RE JUST IN TIME, GIRLS.

BEFORE CLASS STARTS, I GOT SOMETHING VERY IMPORTANT TO ASK YOU...

!

SO, I WANT TO GIVE MY GIRLFRIEND A DRESS FOR HER BIRTHDAY. SINCE I DON'T KNOW MUCH ABOUT IT, I'D LIKE FOR YOU TO GIVE ME YOUR OPINION...

TELL ME, BUT HONESTLY, OKAY? IT'S GREAT, ISN'T IT?

!

UH...

UH...

IT'S ORIGINAL IN ANY CASE...

IT'S BECAUSE I DESIGNED IT AND SEWED IT MYSELF!

OH!

THAT EXPLAINS EVERYTHING!

MAYBE I WASN'T TOTALLY WRONG AFTER ALL! EVEN IF HE DIDN'T STEAL THE DRESS, SAM IS STILL GUILTY OF A CRIME. A FASHION CRIME!

THE FOLLOWING DAYS, THE BALLET REHEARSALS COME ONE AFTER ANOTHER...

AGAIN!

AGAIN AND AGAIN!

IN EACH CLASS, EVERYONE WORKS AT SUCH A SUSTAINED RHYTHM...

AGAIN!

AGAIN!

...THAT BY THE END OF THE WEEK, SOME PEOPLE START LOSING IT...

AGAIN!

AG-- ≥GARGLLL≤...

≥KOF! ≥KOF!

MISS ANNE'S REALLY UNLUCKY!

WITH ALL THESE REHEARSALS, SHE'S LOST HER VOICE!

AGAIN!

AND ONE DAY...

⋛WHEW!⋚ I'VE NEVER DANCED SO MUCH IN MY LIFE!

I'M EXHAUSTED!

IT'S LIKE I SEE DANCING EVERYWHERE!...

EVEN IN MY DREAMS AT NIGHT.

I THINK A LITTLE REST WOULD DO ME GOOD...

GOOD AFTERNOON, EVERYONE!

GOOD AFTERNOON, JULIE!

?!

RUB RUB

SOMETHING WRONG, JULIE?

UH... NO! NO, EVERYTHING'S FINE.

YES! I REALLY DO NEED SOME REST!

WE HAVE AFRICAN DANCE TODAY! THAT'LL BE A CHANGE FOR US FROM CLASSICAL DANCE REHEARSALS.

? ?!

SAM! IS THAT A CARDIGAN?

DO YOU LIKE IT?

MY GIRLFRIEND KNITTED IT FOR ME, TO THANK ME FOR THE DRESS I GAVE HER FOR HER BIRTHDAY...

I DON'T KNOW WHY, BUT SHE TOTALLY INSISTED ON ME WEARING IT!

⸗FFFF!⸗ ⸗FFFF!⸗

THAT'S NOT VERY NICE, BUT YOU CAN UNDERSTAND HER!

HE MADE OUT OKAY. SOME GUYS GET DUMPED FOR LESS THAN THAT!

HEY, GIRLS! I WENT BY THE COSTUME STORAGE TO FIND A HEADBAND FOR MY HAIR...

...AND THE SNOW QUEEN DRESS WASN'T THERE! DO YOU THINK THAT'S NORMAL?

! !

TWO HOURS LATER...

TOM

GOOD JOB, GIRLS! NOW, BEFORE YOU LEAVE, ALL OF YOU STRETCH OUT AND RELAX A FEW MOMENTS...

I CAN'T STOP THINKING ABOUT THAT DRESS DISAPPEARING AGAIN.

ME, EITHER.

ME, EITHER.

WE CAN'T EVEN ACCUSE CARLA ANOTHER TIME. WE HAVE NO PROOF.

OH, YOU KNOW, SHE MUST BE GETTING USED TO IT.

I THINK WE SHOULD START OUR INVESTIGATION BEFORE TALKING TO THE TEACHERS. I'M SURE WE COULD FIND THE DRESS AGAIN.

GOOD IDEA, JULIE!

OKAY, SO WHERE DO WE START?

WELL...

MAYBE BY CLEARING THE ROOM? I HAVE A HIP-HOP CLASS TO TEACH.

!

!

!

YESTERDAY, I BROUGHT SOME STUFF TO THE STORAGE ROOM AFTER REHEARSALS, AND THE DRESS WAS IN ITS PLACE. IF SOMEONE STOLE IT, IT COULD ONLY HAVE BEEN LATER IN THE EVENING.

LET'S GO SEE, NATHALIA. WITH THE PERFORMANCE COMING UP, SHE'S BEEN STAYING LATE TO DO SEWING WORK. MAYBE SHE NOTICED SOMETHING OUT OF THE ORDINARY.

GOOD IDE LUCIE!

LAST NIGHT... HMM... I ONLY SAW CARLA WALKING IN THE HALLWAY, BY HERSELF, AFTER CLASSES...

OH?

THAT POOR CARLA REALLY HAS NO LUCK! SHE'S ALWAYS IN THE WRONG PLACE AT THE WRONG TIME.

HEY, THERE'S MARY! LET'S ASK HER, JUST IN CASE...

NO, I DIDN'T SEE ANYBODY.

OH, YES, I DID! CARLA WAS HANGING AROUND BY THE COSTUME STORAGE!

!

IT IS TROUBLING...

I KNOW SOMEONE ELSE WHO COULD TELL US!

YES, LAST NIGHT, I SAW CARLA LEAVING WITH A PACKAGE UNDER HER ARM. SHE WAS ACTING A LITTLE WEIRD, TOO.

?!?!

EVERYTHING'S POINTING TO CARLA!

LIKE USUAL!

I'LL GO BY AND SEE HER AT HER HOME TO CLARIFY MATTERS.

GO TO CARLA'S?! BUT AREN'T YOU AFRAID THAT MIGHT BE DANGEROUS?

YES?

HELLO, MA'AM. I CAME TO SEE CARLA.

OH? ...UH... COME IN! SHE... SHE'S IN HER ROOM.

IIIIII'M THE SNOOOOOW QUEEEEN!

I'M THE--

NOK NOK

YES?

CARLA, A FRIEND'S COME TO SEE YOU! THAT'S... UNUSUAL, ISN'T IT?

!!

YOU NO DOUBT HAVE LOTS TO TALK ABOUT.

I'LL LET YOU CHAT!

THAT'S THE FIRST TIME CARLA'S HAD A FRIEND OVER. I'LL HAVE TO MAKE THIS SPECIAL.

SO YOU ARE THE ONE WHO TOOK THE SNOW QUEEN DRESS! THIS TIME YOU CAN'T SAY OTHERWISE!

YES! BUT IT'S NOT WHAT YOU THINK, JULIE!

I TOOK THE DRESS TO KEEP IT SAFE UNTIL THE DAY OF THE SHOW.

I DIDN'T WANT SOMEONE TO STEAL IT AGAIN AND FOR ME TO GET BLAMED WHEN I HADN'T DONE ANYTHING.

FOR SURE WE CAN'T WRONGLY ACCUSE YOU THIS TIME SINCE YOU REALLY ARE GUILTY. GOOD THINKING, CARLA!

BUT I SWEAR TO YOU I'D HAVE BROUGHT IT BACK TOMORROW MORNING BEFORE THE FIRST PERFORMANCE.

WELL, BRING IT BACK RIGHT NOW, AND I WON'T TELL ANYONE!

OH, ALL RIGHT! BUT DON'T COMPLAIN IF SOME ILL-INTENTIONED PERSON STEALS IT OVERNIGHT.

NOW I JUST HAVE TO LET LUCIE AND ALIA KNOW EVERYTHING'S BEEN SETTLED...

OH! YOU'RE LEAVING ALREADY?

AND I'D FIXED A SIMPLE, LITTLE SNACK FOR YOU TWO...

PARTY TIME

?

?!

THAT NIGHT...

WHEN'S THE BEGINNING OF THE SHOW, JULIE? I CAN'T WAIT TO BE THERE!

TOMORROW EVENING, CAPUCINE!

THE NEXT DAY...

AND HOW LONG WILL IT BE NOW?

ABOUT... TEN HOURS, CAPUCINE!

FIVE HOURS TO GO, CAPUCINE!

⇒PFFF!⇐ IT'S REALLY NOT GOING BY VERY FAST!

IT'S IN TWO HOURS, CAPUCINE!

THAT LONG?

WHEN EVENING COMES, AT THE CITY THEATER...

ONLY AN HOUR LEFT BEFORE THE BEGINNING OF THE SHOW!

AAAAAH!

THE SNOW QUEEN

ARE YOU READY, GIRLS? YOU GO ON STAGE IN TEN MINUTES!

!

TEN MINUTES! IT'S HORRIBLE! I'VE GOT STAGE FRIGHT!

I DON'T WANT TO GO OUT THERE! ⇒BOOOOOO-HOOOOO!⇐

?!

- 37 -

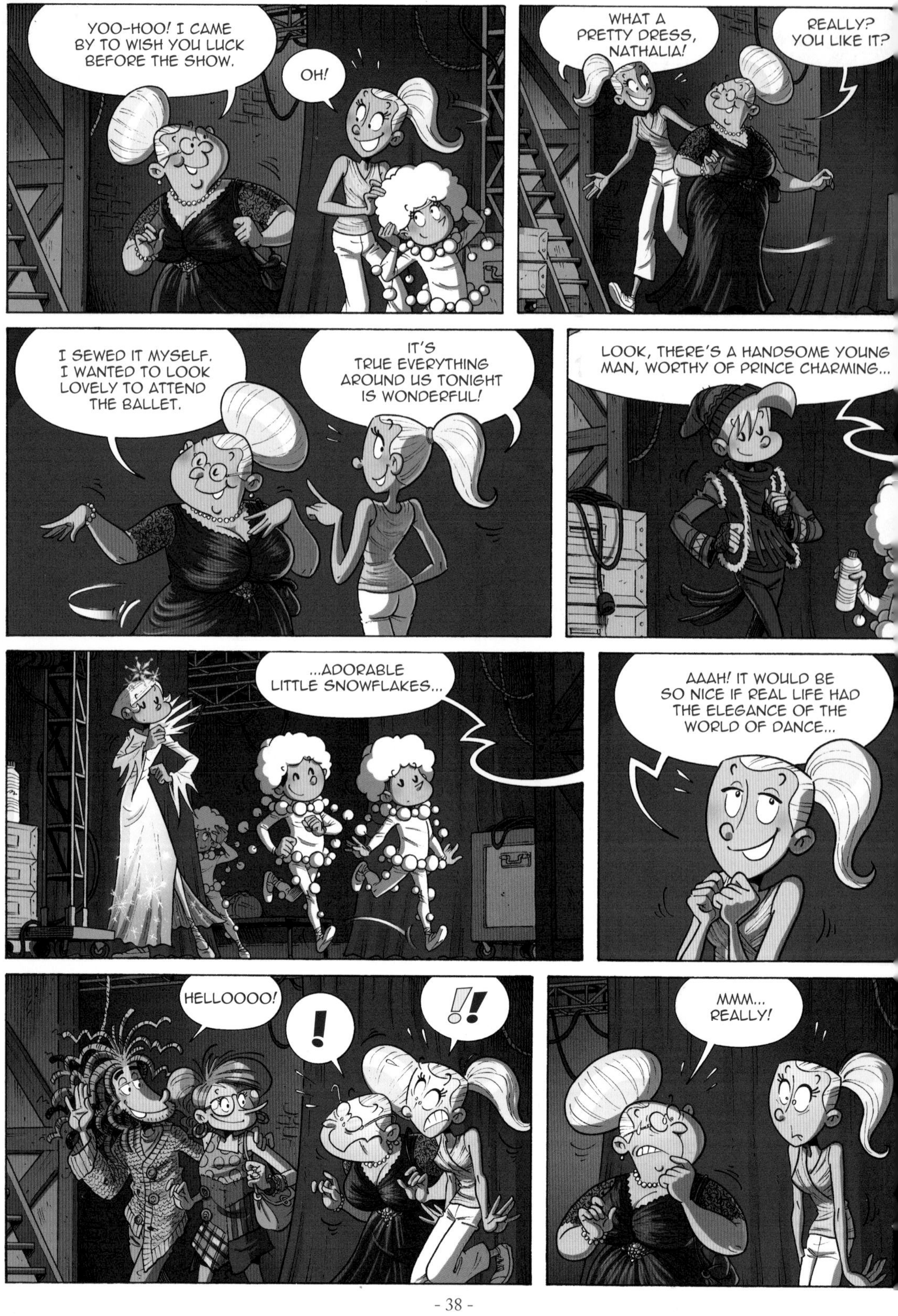
YOO-HOO! I CAME BY TO WISH YOU LUCK BEFORE THE SHOW.
OH!
WHAT A PRETTY DRESS, NATHALIA!
REALLY? YOU LIKE IT?
I SEWED IT MYSELF. I WANTED TO LOOK LOVELY TO ATTEND THE BALLET.
IT'S TRUE EVERYTHING AROUND US TONIGHT IS WONDERFUL!
LOOK, THERE'S A HANDSOME YOUNG MAN, WORTHY OF PRINCE CHARMING...
...ADORABLE LITTLE SNOWFLAKES...
AAAH! IT WOULD BE SO NICE IF REAL LIFE HAD THE ELEGANCE OF THE WORLD OF DANCE...
HELLOOOO!
!
!!
MMM... REALLY!

SCENE 1:

THE FEARSOME SNOW QUEEN IS BORED AND LONELY IN HER ICE PALACE. ONE DAY, SHE DECIDES TO ABDUCT A YOUNG MAN TO MAKE HIM HER KING. AT THE SAME TIME, GERDA AND KAY, TWO YOUNG LOVERS, HAVE A RENDEZVOUS NOT FAR FROM THEIR VILLAGE...

SO, DID YOU LIKE THAT FIRST SCENE? I WAS GOOD, RIGHT?

CLAP CLAP

CLAP CLAP

?

SINCE I WON'T DANCE AGAIN FOR A LITTLE BIT, I'LL BE ABLE TO EXPLAIN EVERYTHING TO YOU!

OH?

THE SNOW QUEEN HAS JUST PUT A SHARD OF ICE IN KAY'S HEART SO HE'LL FORGET GERDA. AFTERWARDS, WITH HER ARMY OF SNOWFLAKES, THE QUEEN TOOK HIM AWAY TO LOCK HIM UP IN HER PALACE!

NOW, YOU'LL SEE! GERDA IS GOING TO DEPART IN SEARCH OF KAY!

IF YOU DON'T UNDERSTAND SOMETHING, JUST ASK ME, OKAY?

UH, OKAY... THANKS, CAPUCINE!

SCENE II:

GERDA IS DEVASTATED. SHE'D LIKE TO GO HELP KAY, BUT SHE TRULY DOESN'T KNOW HOW TO DO SO...

DID YOU UNDERSTAND, DADDY? CARROT THE SNOWMAN IS GOING TO ACCOMPANY GERDA TO THE LAND OF ICE TO HELP FREE KAY!

THE LAND OF ICE... THAT MAKES ME THINK I'D GLADLY EAT AN ESKIMO PIE!

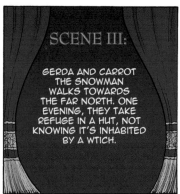

SCENE III:

GERDA AND CARROT THE SNOWMAN WALKS TOWARDS THE FAR NORTH. ONE EVENING, THEY TAKE REFUGE IN A HUT, NOT KNOWING IT'S INHABITED BY A WTICH.

THE WITCH HAS JUST ENCHANTED THE FLOWER SO IT WILL MELT THE SHARD OF ICE IN KAY'S HEART...

CLAP CLAP

CLAP CLAP

YOU KNOW, A LITTLE LIKE WHEN YOU GIVE MOMMY FLOWERS AFTER AN ARGUMENT!

CLAP CLAP

SCENE IV:

GERDA AND CARROT THE SNOWMAN ARRIVE IN THE LAND OF THE SNOW QUEEN...

NOW YOU'LL SEE! THE SNOW QUEEN WILL SEND HER ARMY OF SNOWFLAKES TO ARREST GERDA AND CARROT. BUT THEY'LL DEFEND THEMSELVES THANKS TO THE MAGIC FLOWER AND...

!!

THE ARMY OF SNOWFLAKES! BUT... I'M PART OF THAT! I GOT TO GO AND QUICK!

!

? ? ? ? ?

?

HEE-HEE... SNOWFLAKE!

AFTER HAVING
CHASED AWAY THE WIND
AND THE SNOWFLAKES,
GERDA AND CARROT
ARRIVE AT THE
SNOW QUEEN'S
ICE PALACE...

I GOT HERE JUST IN TIME TO EXPLAIN THE FINALE TO YOU!

GERDA HAS FREED KAY FROM THE SPELL, AND THE SNOW QUEEN FINDS HERSELF ALL ALONE AGAIN!

SINCE THEN, SHE'S SO FURIOUS THAT, EVERY YEAR, SHE SENDS A TERRIBLE WINTER TO THE WORLD OF HUMANS TO GET REVENGE...

BRAVO!

ENCORE!

BRAVO!

BUT MAYBE SHE DIDN'T PLAN ON GLOBAL WARMING!

CLAP CLAP

CLAP CLAP CLAP

CLAP CLAP

CLAP CLAP CLAP

I THINK WE REALLY DANCED WELL!

YES, EVERYTHING WAS PERFECT.

!

HEY! I WAS PUTTING AWAY THE COSTUMES AND GUESS WHAT? THE SHOW QUEEN'S DRESS HAS DISAPPEARED!

AGAIN?

NO WAY!

AHHHH! I'M FREE, FREE OF ALL SUSPICION!

I WAS ON STAGE GETTING APPLAUDED!

I WONDER WHO COULD'VE TAKEN IT THIS TIME?

I'LL QUICKLY GO PUT THIS SNOW QUEEN'S DRESS IN A SAFE PLACE!

IT'D BE AWFUL IF IT DISAPPEARED AGAIN!

END

WATCH OUT FOR PAPERCUTZ ™

Welcome to the toe-tapping tenth DANCE CLASS graphic novel by Crip & Béka, and Maëla Cosson, from Papercutz, those frosty folks dedicated to publishing great graphic novels for all ages. I'm Jim Salicrup, the Editor-in-Chief of Papercutz and semi-regular viewer of *Dancing with the Stars*, here to point out something unique about DANCE CLASS…

Ready? Here it is… There are no cats in DANCE CLASS.

You may be wondering what's the big deal about no cats in DANCE CLASS. So, allow me to explain. Seems that there are so many cats featured in Papercutz graphic novels, that it's often suggested that we change our name to *Papercatz*. Now it's spreading to Charmz! Obviously, we must love cats. Here's a list of just some of the other cats you'll find published by Papercutz…

Azrael – This naughty kitty belongs to the Smurfs's archfoe, Gargamel. Azrael would love nothing better than to eat a Smurf! You can find Azrael in THE SMURFS graphic novels by Peyo.

Brina – A two-year-old city cat, named Brina, takes a summer vacation in the country with her owners. Here she meets a group of stray cats who call themselves "The Gang of the Feline Sun," who convince her to run away with them and live life as a free cat. While Brina enjoys her newfound freedom and all the new delectable bugs the countryside has to offer, her young owners are distraught over losing her, someone they consider a member of their family. Brina is terribly conflicted and must choose to return to her owners or to continue to live free in the wild. We think you'll love Brina as much as we do, so don't miss BRINA THE CAT #1 "The Gang of the Feline Sun" by Giorgio Salati and Christian Cornia

Cartoon – Is a pretty happy cat, and he lives with Chloe and her family. CHLOE, by Greg Tessier (writer) and Amandine (artist) is published by Charmz, a Papercutz imprint focused on young love. Even though Cartoon is a minor character in CHLOE, he's proven so popular that he's now co-starring in CHLOE & CARTOON #1!

Cliff – Is the pet cat of the Loud family and is just one of the many occupants of THE LOUD HOUSE. There's Lincoln Loud, his ten sisters (Lori, Leni, Luna, Luan, Lynn, Lucy, Lisa, Lola, Lana, and Lily), his parents (Rita and Lynn Sr.), and the other pets, Charles (a dog), El Diablo (a snake), Hops (a frog), Walt (a bird), and Geo (a hamster). Cliff may not be the star of THE LOUD HOUSE, but the fact is that the Nickelodeon animated series is a big hit, as are the Papercutz graphic novels, so who's to say he's not a part of what's making THE LOUD HOUSE so successful?

Hubble – Is the snarky pet cat of the Monroe family, and the unofficial mascot of the GEEKY F@B 5. Hubble has watched sisters Lucy and Marina Monroe, start up the Geeky F@b 5 with their friends, Zara, A.J., and Sofia, and tackle all sorts of problems, including finding homes for pets when the local animal shelter suffers major damage from a tornado. Even Hubble must admit that when girls stick together, anything is possible! Written by mother/daughter writing team, Liz & Lucy Lareau, and drawn by artist Ryan Jampole.

Pussycat – Before Peyo created THE SMURFS he wrote and drew the adventures of PUSSYCAT. Pussycat is a lovable, mischievous tuxedo cat who spends his time chasing after milk and snacks and framing other members of his family for his shenanigans Warning: our hero Pussycat is a real cat. He does not speak (he just meows) and his main passions in life are eating, hunting mice, avoiding dogs and meowing at night. All of Pussycat's adventures are, collected in one deluxe volume entitled, PUSSYCAT.

Scarlett – Scarlett, as revealed in SCARLETT "Star on the Run" by Jon Buller (author/artist) and Susan Schade (author/artist), is a small, harlequin-colored cat and a huge movie star. And what's more — she talks! Unfortunately, she's also abused by her producer, so she dreams of only one thing: escaping! When the occasion presents itself, she runs for her life.

Sushi – In CAT AND CAT by Christophe Cazenove (co-writer), Herve Richez (co-writer), and Yrgane Ramon (artist), when Sushi is adopted by Cat (short for Catherine) and her dad, their quiet life of living alone is over. Between turning everything into either a personal scratching post or litter box, and the constant cat and mouse game of "love me/leave me alone," Sushi convinces Cat and her dad that they have a lot to learn about cats.

Sybil – Is the cute cat owned by fourteen-year-old (soon to be fifteen) Amy Von Brandt. Amy's life is never dull, and you can find out all about her and Sybil in AMY'S DIARY by Véronique Grisseaux (writer) and Laëtitia Ayné (artist), based on the novels by India Desjardins, and published by Charmz.

We could go on and on, but we think you get the point! (We didn't even mention Geronimo Stilton's purr-sistant foes, the Pirate Cats, who in the GERONIMO STILTON graphic novels, are always trying to rewrite history to their advantage!) Instead, we'll just ask you to keep an eye out for the next DANCE CLASS graphic novel, and to watch out for Papercutz… and Charmz!

Thanks, *JIM*

STAY IN TOUCH!

EMAIL: salicrup@papercutz.com
WEB: www.papercutz.com
TWITTER: @papercutzgn
FACEBOOK: PAPERCUTZGRAPHICNOVELS
MAIL: Papercutz, 160 Broadway, Suite 700, East Wing, New York, NY 10038

MORE GREAT GRAPHIC NOVEL SERIES AVAILABLE FROM
PAPERCUTZ™

THE SMURFS

ASTERIX

DANCE CLASS

THE SISTERS

CAT & CAT

GERONIMO STILTON

GERONIMO STILTON REPORTER

MELOWY

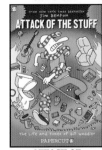

DINOSAUR EXPLORERS

ATTACK OF THE STUFF

THE MYTHICS

FUZZY BASEBALL

THE RED SHOES

THE LITTLE MERMAID

BLUEBEARD

HOTEL TRANSYLVANIA

THE LOUD HOUSE

GUMBY

THE ONLY LIVING BOY

THE ONLY LIVING GIRL

Go to papercutz.com for more information
Also available where ebooks are sold.